Note to parents, carers and teachers

Read it yourself is a series of modern stories, favourite characters and traditional tales written in a simple way for children who are learning to read. The books can be read independently or as part of a guided reading session.

Each book is carefully structured to include many high-frequency words vital for first reading. The sentences on each page are supported closely by pictures to help with understanding, and to offer lively details to talk about.

The books are graded into four levels that progressively introduce wider vocabulary and longer stories as a reader's ability and confidence grows.

Ideas for use

- Begin by looking through the book and talking about the pictures. Has your child heard this story before?

- Help your child with any words he does not know, either by helping him to sound them out or supplying them yourself.

- Developing readers can be concentrating so hard on the words that they sometimes don't fully grasp the meaning of what they're reading. Answering the puzzle questions at the end of the book will help with understanding.

For more information and advice on Read it yourself and book banding, visit **www.ladybird.com/readityourself**

Book Band 6

Level 2 is ideal for children who have received some reading instruction and can read short, simple sentences with help.

Special features:

Frequent repetition of main story words and phrases

Peppa, George, Mummy Pig and Daddy Pig are going on holiday.

"Look!" says Peppa. "Here's Daddy!"

"Hooray!" says Mummy Pig. "And look, he has a camper van!"

Short, simple sentences

6

7

Large, clear type

"Look!" says Mummy Pig. "We are here!"

"Hooray!" says Peppa.

Careful match between story and pictures

20

21

Educational Consultant: Geraldine Taylor
Book Banding Consultant: Kate Ruttle

LADYBIRD BOOKS

UK | USA | Canada | Ireland | Australia
India | New Zealand | South Africa

Ladybird Books is part of the Penguin Random House group of companies
whose addresses can be found at global.penguinrandomhouse.com.

www.penguin.co.uk   www.puffin.co.uk   www.ladybird.co.uk

Penguin
Random House
UK

Text adapted from Peppa Goes Camping, first published by Ladybird Books, 2010
This version first published by Ladybird Books, 2015
003

This book is based on the
TV Series 'Peppa Pig'
'Peppa Pig' is created by
Neville Astley and Mark Baker
Peppa Pig © Astley Baker Davies Ltd/
Entertainment One UK Ltd, 2003

www.peppapig.com

Printed in China

A CIP catalogue record for this book is
available from the British Library

ISBN: 978-0-723-29529-7

MIX
Paper from
responsible sources
FSC® C018179

Camping Trip

Adaptation written by Lorraine Horsley
Based on the TV series 'Peppa Pig'. 'Peppa Pig' is
created by Neville Astley and Mark Baker

Peppa, George, Mummy Pig
and Daddy Pig are going
on holiday.

"Look!" says Peppa.
"Here's Daddy!"

"Hooray!" says Mummy.
"And look, he has a
camper van!"

They all jump in the camper van.

"Off we go!" says Daddy.

"We are going on holiday!" sings Peppa. "We are going on holiday in our camper van!"

But Daddy Pig is lost.

Along comes Grandad Dog.

"Can you help us?"
asks Peppa. "We are lost!"

"Have you looked at
your satnav?" asks
Grandad Dog.

"What is a satnav?" asks
Daddy Pig.

"A satnav helps you find your
way," says Grandad Dog.

He looks in the camper
van and finds the satnav
for Daddy. The satnav tells
Daddy the way to go.

"We are going on holiday!"
sings Peppa. "We are
going on holiday in our
camper van!"

But the camper van
is out of oil.

15

Daddy Pig looks for the engine, but he cannot find it.

Along comes Mummy Sheep.

"Can you help us?" asks Peppa. "We cannot find our engine."

16

Mummy Sheep finds the engine in the back of the camper van.

Daddy Pig puts oil in the engine and off they go!

"Look!" says Mummy Pig.
"We are here!"

"Hooray!" says Peppa.

"Time for bed!" says Mummy Pig.

"But what about our beds?" asks Peppa. "Our beds are back at home!"

"Just look here," Daddy Pig tells Peppa, and he presses a big button.

Out comes a big bed
for Mummy Pig and
Daddy Pig.

Daddy Pig presses a
little button.

"And here are your beds,"
he says.

This time, two little beds come out for Peppa and George.

George and Peppa jump into the little beds.

"I like this camper van!"
says Peppa. "It is just
like home!"

"Goodnight!" says
the satnav.

Goodnight!" says Peppa.

29

How much do you remember about Peppa Pig: Camping Trip? Answer these questions and find out!

- What does Daddy Pig use to help find the way to go?

- Who helps find the camper van's engine?

- What does Daddy Pig put in the engine to make it go?

- How do they find the beds in the camper van?

Look at the pictures and match them to the story words.

camper van

Daddy Pig

satnav

engine

Mummy Sheep

Tick the books you've read!

Level 2

Level 3

The Read it yourself with Ladybird app is now available